THE Mismatched NATIVITY

To Mom, who began our family tradition
of collecting nativity sets from
around the world.
—MB

For my mom, Ann.
—ST

Text © 2016 Merrilee Boyack

Illustrations © 2016 Shawna J. C. Tenney

Visit us at DeseretBook.com

Library of Congress Cataloging-in-Publication Data

Names: Boyack, Merrilee Browne, author. | Tenney, Shawna J. C., illustrator.
Title: The mismatched nativity / text by Merrilee Boyack ; Illustrated by Shawna Tenney.
Description: Salt Lake City, Utah : Deseret Book, [2016] | Summary: A young boy who has just moved to a new town at Christmastime feels lonely, but makes new friends in his Primary class when they create a nativity set for him.
Identifiers: LCCN 2016006460 | ISBN 9781629722399 (hardbound : alk. paper)
Subjects: | CYAC: Friendship—Fiction. | Moving, Household—Fiction. | Creches (Nativity scenes)—Fiction. | Christmas—Fiction. | Mormons—Fiction. | The Church of Jesus Christ of Latter-day Saints—Fiction.
Classification: LCC PZ7.1.B69 Wh 2015 | DDC [E]—dc23
LC record available at http://lccn.loc.gov/2016006460

Printed in China
Production Date: 2019-08-01
Job / Batch#: 84728
Plant & Location: Printed by Everbest Printing (Guangzhou, China), Co. Ltd

10 9 8 7 6 5 4 3 2

THE
Mismatched
NATIVITY

Written by
Merrilee Boyack

Illustrated by
Shawna J. C. Tenney

DESERET
BOOK

Salt Lake City, Utah

Joshua was new to his class at church and he was feeling pretty lonely. The teacher, Sister Bennett, welcomed him and asked him to say hello.

"Hello," he said quietly, staring at the floor and running his fingers through his dark hair.

"Joshua has moved here from across the country," Sister Bennett said. She smiled at Josh and said, "We're happy you're in our class. I think you're going to like it here."

Joshua was silent for the rest of the lesson.

The next week Joshua was not in church. Sister Bennett said to the class, "Can you imagine how hard it would be to move somewhere far away? Joshua could really use some love and friendship. Christmas is coming soon. What do you think about showing him that we're glad he's here?"

Sister Bennett explained, "I have an idea about how we could show Josh that he has friends who care about him. You will need to ask your parents for their help and permission, but I think there is something we can do to give Josh a happy Christmas in his new home."

The next afternoon, Sammy stopped by Joshua's house with his dog. "Hey, Josh! Want to go for a walk with me and my dog?" Sammy asked. Joshua smiled and agreed. He liked dogs. Sammy's dog was big and golden and had a long tail that bounced happily in the air.

Joshua put on his coat and gloves, and the boys took turns with the leash as they walked the dog through the neighborhood. When they got back to Joshua's house, Sammy handed him a small shepherd figurine. Josh held it in his hands and rubbed his hands over the brown wood.

"My mom said I could give you this from one of our nativity sets," Sammy said. "I like the shepherds because they took care of their sheep like I take care of my dog."

Josh said thank you and set the small wooden shepherd, holding a strong, curved staff, on the table by the door.

A few days later, Maria knocked on Joshua's door. "Hi, Joshua," she said. "I'm Maria—from your Primary class. I brought you a treat!" She held out a plate of Christmas cookies shaped like stars and a container of frosting. "Want to help me frost them?" she asked.

After more than a little nibbling and finger licking, they had artfully decorated the cookies with mounds of frosting and colorful candy sprinkles.

"I brought you a star from our nativity set," Maria said when it was time for her to go home. "My mom said you could have it."

Josh held up the shiny gold star. He put it across from the shepherd on the table by the door. "Cool," he said. "Now the shepherd will know what direction to go!"

On Saturday, Taylor called across the fence to Josh, who was playing in his backyard. "Want to help me build a birdhouse? I'm making it for my mom for Christmas."

Josh climbed over the fence to Taylor's backyard. They worked all afternoon carefully gluing and hammering the pieces together. When they were finished, they were both proud of the birdhouse they had made.

"Wait," Taylor said, handing Joshua something as he started to climb back over the fence. "I made this for you. It will remind you of building the birdhouse together."

It was a small manger with short pieces of straw tucked inside to make a bed.

"Thanks!" Joshua said. Back at home, he set the manger next to the shepherd on the table by the door.

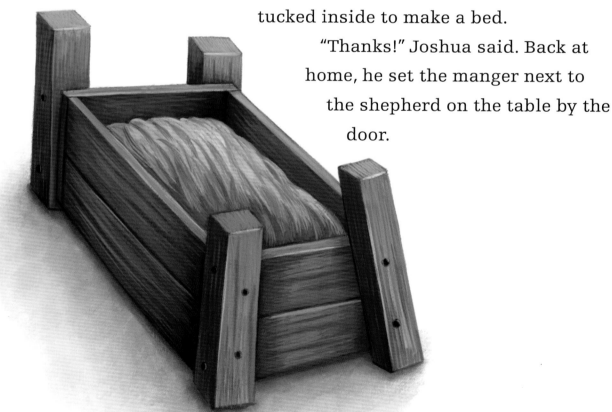

The next week, Keaton came to the front door. "Can you go sledding with me and my dad?" he asked.

Off they went to the park, where Josh slid down the hill over and over with Keaton and his father. As they were driving home, Keaton reached into a sack sitting on the back seat. He handed Josh a tall figure. "This is Joseph from our nativity set," he said. "He reminds me of my dad because Joseph was good to baby Jesus and helped him."

Joshua liked the tall figure with the kind face and tan robe, holding a small lantern in one hand. He placed Joseph by the manger and the shepherd.

The next day, Holly caught up with Josh on the way home from school. "Hi, Josh! Do you want to come over and help us decorate our Christmas tree?"

The children spent the rest of the afternoon hanging ornaments and stringing popcorn. When they were finished, Holly handed Joshua a porcelain figure of a pretty woman with long hair and a simple blue robe.

"This is Mary," Holly said. "She's my favorite nativity piece. Someday I want to be a mommy like her."

Josh thanked her and went home to put Mary next to Joseph on the table.

A few days later, Angela rang the doorbell. "Can you come out and play in the snow?" she asked. Joshua pulled on his boots and together they walked up the snow-packed sidewalk to Angela's house. With the help of Angela's three older brothers, they made three fat snowmen with big carrots stuck into their heads for noses.

When they were finished, the children gathered around Joshua. "We have a gift for you from our family," Angela said. She handed him three wise men. "These are like my big brothers."

"And like our snowmen!" one of the boys added.

Joshua loved the colorful wise men with jewels and crowns and small packages. "Thanks a lot!" He smiled and gently carried the wise men home to sit on the table with the other figures.

On Christmas Eve, Joshua and his parents examined
their nativity set. Josh told his family about the
things he had done with each of his new friends. Just
then, the doorbell rang. On the porch stood Sister Bennett,
Joshua's Primary teacher.

H i, Josh!" Sister Bennett said. "I brought you a present!"

Joshua's father invited her to come inside.

"Well, that's quite an interesting nativity set," she said, looking at the table by the door. "But it is missing someone pretty important."

Sister Bennett held out her hand to Josh, revealing a little figurine. "Here's the baby Jesus for your nativity set!" she said. "This is the most important part. This will remind you that Jesus loves you very much!"

Joshua put the little baby Jesus in the manger. Now his set was complete.

The doorbell rang again, and this time Joshua opened the door to find lots of people gathered on the front porch.

"Hi, Josh!" his friends from church called. "We've come to spend Christmas Eve with you!" Juggling plates of food and treats, his friends and their families made their way inside.

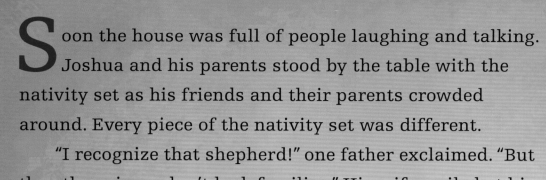

Soon the house was full of people laughing and talking. Joshua and his parents stood by the table with the nativity set as his friends and their parents crowded around. Every piece of the nativity set was different.

"I recognize that shepherd!" one father exclaimed. "But the other pieces don't look familiar." His wife smiled at him.

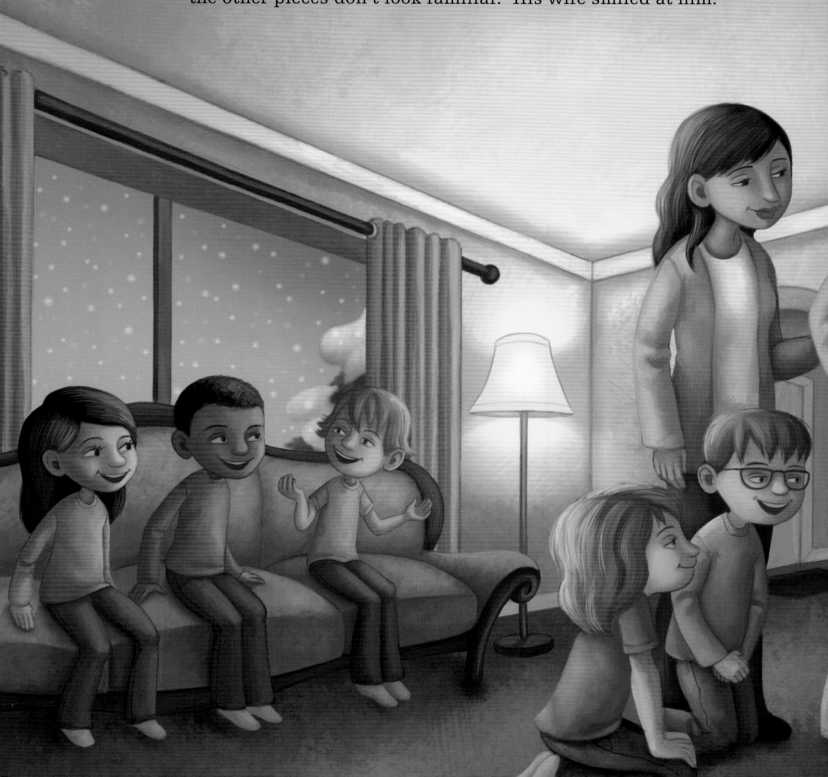

"I made the manger!" Taylor exclaimed.

"And we added the wise men!" Angela said.

"I think this is right where they belong," her mother observed.

That's a pretty mismatched nativity set!" said one of the parents.

"It's true," agreed Joshua, "but I think it's the most beautiful nativity set in the whole world."

"It sure is," Joshua's mom said. "That nativity set shows us what Jesus taught us—that we should love one another."

Suggestions for Parents

Christmas activities focused on the nativity are a fun way for help teach children about the story of Christ's birth. At the end of each activity, you could make, color, or purchase an element of the nativity scene for your children to remember the activity.

Shepherd: Arrange for your children to care for a pet or farm animal. Perhaps they could take the pet for a walk, give it a special treat, or take a turn grooming it. You might take your children to a farm, zoo, or local animal shelter. Talk about how a shepherd cares for his sheep and how Jesus cares for each of us. Find scriptures that contain the word *shepherd*.

Star: Make cookies and decorate them to give to a neighbor. You could have your children cut the shape of a star out of cardboard and wrap it in foil to hang from their bedroom ceilings. Another option would be to purchase glow-in-the-dark stars and stick them to the ceiling. Talk about how the shepherds followed the star to see Jesus and how each of us needs to follow Jesus and believe in Him. Find the verses in 3 Nephi that talk about the new star.

Manger: Help your children make a manger out of a small box or build one with wood. Place a small pile of straw next to the manger and your children put in one piece of straw each time they perform an act of kindness. Talk about how we make room for Jesus in our lives by thinking of Him each day and by serving and loving others as He did.

Joseph: Arrange for your children to spend time with a male role model, such as a father, grandfather, uncle, older brother, or home teacher. Talk about Joseph and what he did to protect Jesus and to take care of his family. Perhaps your children could do a woodworking project to learn how Jesus was taught carpentry by Joseph.

Mary: To celebrate Mary's special role, arrange to have your children spend time with a baby. You could visit a baby in your congregation, neighborhood, or family and have the mother show your children some of the things she does to care for the baby. Take a picture of your children with the baby. Talk about Mary's role in caring for Jesus and explain her sacrifice. Discuss how we can focus our lives on Jesus.

Wise men: Help your children make Christmas gifts that they can give to others. There are many simple ideas available on the Internet using items that are readily available at home. Discuss with your

children the importance of giving gifts. Read the scripture story about the visit of the wise men and how they helped Jesus's family with their gifts. Talk about how sharing gifts is sharing love with others.

Baby Jesus: Have your children frame or color a picture of the nativity to put in their bedrooms. Talk about the story of Jesus's birth and how He learned and grew. Help your children set goals of behaviors they can work on in their lives to become more like Jesus. Have them put a star sticker around the edge of the picture for every day they work on their goals.